ROCCO VS MOON

CAROLA JOTHI

Copyright © 2019 by Carola Jothi.

ISBN   978-1-970160-52-9   Ebook
ISBN   978-1-970160-53-6   Paperback

All rights reserved. No part of this publication may be reproduced, distributed, or transmitted in any form or by any means, including photocopying, recording, or other electronic or mechanical methods without the prior written permission of the publisher. For permission requests, solicit the publisher via the address below through mail or email with the subject line "Attention: Publication Permission".

EC Publishing LLC
11100 SW 93rd Court Road, Suite 10-215
Ocala, Florida 34481-5188, USA

Ordering Information:
Quantity sales. Special discounts are available on quantity purchases by corporations, associations, and others. For details, contact the publisher at the address above.

www.ecpublishingllc.com
info@ecpublishingllc.com
+1 (352) 234-6201

Printed in the United States of America

DEDICATION

I want to thank my family. Jana, Gonzalo and Maria to inspire me to write. Being there for me. Bad and good days. I couldn't have done it without you. Entering into your life was the best thing. felt like I was reborn to a new family second chance. You made me a better person.

Carola Jothi

CHAPTER 1

The earth is spinning, trees are changing, and animals are hiding. People are looking for a safe cover.

Rocco is standing in the woods, watching Moon. He knew Moon was much stronger. He wasn't ready to fight her just yet. He needs to build an army and find a place for him to start a war and to take over.

Rocco takes off.

Rocco is developing more powers and destroying everything he touches and on his way. As he keeps going, he finds villages and some army.

He tells the army "Join me and I will give you anything you want!" The army looked at him crazily. The leader of the army told him "Leave! You don't belong here. " Rocco warned the leader and said "Join me and I will let you live! "

The army pulled out their weapons and pointed at Rocco.

Rocco says, "very well, if that's the way you want to play. "

Rocco was not scared at all. He knew he have powers and he will use it to rule the world.

He took his hand, clapped twice and said, "Let the strong wind blow the army into the trees." some lived and some died.

The leader of the army bowed down and said, "We are yours."

Rocco smiled and took over the army.

He kept on going and going until he found a place to hide and gather more armies along the way.

Moon, dreaming in her sleep… trees on fire, people screaming. In the fire, a new creature that has never been seen before was created by a man.

Moon woke up, heart beating fast and breathing heavily. She got up and walked to the mirror and said, "It's just a dream."

Olazon knocked at the door.

Moon said, Eenter. What is it?"

Olazon: "You must come see this!"

Moon rushed out and saw an army with a red flag.

She told Olazon to warn everyone and to release the animals. Moon commanded "Gather some warriors and follow me!"

Olazon warned the others and gathered warriors to follow the queen.

Moon and her warriors marched toward the army of red flag.

Moon and her warriors are standing behind the bridge. She yells, who are you and what do you want?!". The red flag armies all yell. Saying "War War War!" Moon answered back "We want peace, turn around and go back where you belong!"

Suddenly the armies stopped yelling. Black figure walking towards the bridge, with his very own big foot, red eyes and a collar on his neck.

Bigfoot roars….. Rocco puts his hand up and silent.

He takes his hood off his head and shouted:

"Moon!

Moon looked at him, shocked. "Not again" she says.

Moon and Rocco are staring at each other. Rocco tells moon

"I will be taking your village and your people and I will kill you."

Moon is silent and told Olazon to sound the alarm. "Release the anaconda one of them! ", she yells.

Rocco saw a huge anaconda coming at them but Rocco also released his own anaconda and starts to move forward.

As two anaconda head to head.

Moon told Olazon to tell his men to fall back now.

Rocco's army shooting spare arrow at moons anaconda.

Moon and her army fall back and planned to attack Rocco's army. She had no choice.

They can hear them coming.

James, Moon and Yeti stayed close to each other. While Olazon and his army are in front guarding them.

Rocco and his army enters the village and started to attack. Blood are splattering. Both armies dying and injured. Animals attacking each other.

Olazon told James and Yeti to take Moon. "There's too many of them. My warriors and I will try to hold them back. Go now!", Olazon said.

James, Yeti and Moon ran out of the village.

James saw moon running in a wrong direction. She was heading to the chamber where the animals were. James and Yeti went after her.

James told moon, "What are you doing. We need to get out of here now!" Moon took 5 eggs with her. James asked, "What the hell is that?

Moon said "You'll see". Yeti roaring. The three of them ran out of the chamber. Running into the woods, Moon turn around and saw Olazon fighting Rocco. And Rocco stabbed Olazon and cut his head off.

Moon yelled loud "Nooooo!"

Rocco heard Moon and told his army, "Go after her and bring her alive back in this village!"

Bigfoot and the few animals of Rocco and his 15 soldiers went after Moon.

Moon, James and Yeti running as far as they can. Some of the animals and Olazon's soldiers have escaped.

Moon found a cave and took 5 eggs. James desperately wants to know what the eggs are. Yeti looking for logs to start fire.

Moon takes out 5 eggs and put it in warm hole. She said to James, "I will tell you what they are. Those 5 eggs are two headed anaconda snakes. We lost one anaconda. I'm not about to lose these ones."

James told Moon, "I must go back, see if I can find our soldiers and the animals and bring them here."

Moon told James not to go. Rocco will have his army and animal looking for them. "We must stay here for the night. Then we leave dawn.", Moon commanded.

Back in the village, Rocco took Moon´s village and explored. He saw the chamber. He goes down into the chamber, saw that it was big and empty.

He told his soldiers, "Bring my creatures and we are going to catch a bird call Bangladesh Crow." A soldier asks, "What's the bird for?" Rocco told him, "You'll see."

Some of the soldiers went out to hunt down a bird for Rocco.

The soldiers return and brought two birds to Rocco. Rocco was pleased.

He told the soldiers to leave. He put the birds in the cage. Rocco touches the birds and gave them a little bottle with red liquid in it. Rocco opened the bird's mouth then close it. The birds passed out. Rocco pet the birds and said "You'll be ok. You will grow big in a few hours."

Rocco and the 5 soldiers return to the chamber and saw a huge bird, the size of a horse.

Rocco tells the bird, "Go get me the queen, bring her to me alive. Kill the rest of the people".

The birds take off. Rocco tells "Mawk", the leader of the soldier "Be my right hand". Mawk said to him, "It would be an honor sir."

Rocco smiled and gets ready for Moon's arrival.

Moon, James and Yeti left the cave. They went back to Yeti's village. Up in the mountains, where all others are.

Moon explains to all "Yeti, we must gather more warriors. War is still coming. Rocco is still alive and he is powerful."

Moon asked the leader Yeti, "Teach how to fight better and be the best fighter!" Yeti bowed and said, "Yes I will teach you."

Moon smiled.

James went up to Moon and asked her to walk with him. Moon accepted and told Yeti that she's going for a walk. James and Moon went for a walk along with Yeti.

James said, "Moon, you must let me fight Rocco. You're not strong enough to fight him."

Moon looked at James and asked, "Is there something you're not telling me?"

James replied "There is something that I do have to tell you about Rocco." Moon said, "Ok but I would like to know how he got powers." James said, "I know how he got powers."

Moon desperately wants to know. Moon instructed two yetis, "Go back to the village. We will be fine. Tell your leader to get everything and everyone ready for tonight. We're leaving tonight. We've must leave the mountain." James and Moon went into the woods and saw a little village that was abandoned. Both went into the village, looked around and stayed in one of the villages.

Dark clouds coming along with thunders, then it starts to rain very hard. James went to get some wood to start a fire.

James and Moon sat down by the fireplace and he starts to tell her how Rocco got powers.

James started to tell the story, "You remember the red diamond?" Moon replied, "Yes I remember." James continued, "Well, when he built a machine. He created two more red diamonds." Moon said, "Wait I remember two red diamonds that I destroyed in the cave. So there was a third red diamond? What happened to the third?"

James replied, "He took the third red diamond and manage to open the inside. Inside was liquid red like a potion. He decided to pour it on his drink and drank it. He didn't have enough to use it on his animals. So he had 3 more drops of the red liquid. He put it in small skinny bottle and took one, for one very special creature he kept hidden. One for himself. The last small bottle. I stole it."

Moon looked at James with curiosity and asked why.

James told her, "I was going to take it for myself to defeat him. You can't win when the enemy is strong and powerful."

James holds Moon's hand, looked into her eyes and said "You should take it to be powerful to defeat Rocco. Kill him, it's your destiny." Moon shook her head "No. There's got to be other ways other than this."

James knew there wasn't any other way and said "Rocco was getting stronger and getting good at his powers."

Moon asked James, "If I take this red formula. I'll never be normal. I'll have powers forever unless I die."

James assured Moon, "You don't have to take it right now. When you're ready. I'll be right beside you all the way.

Moon starts to fall in love with James.

Back in the village, Rocco has been patiently waiting for the bird to return. But nothing. He decided to grab some army and a few animals with him to go on hunting. Rocco thinks he knew where Moon could be. And so he went.

James and Moon loving one another. Moon looked over at James sleeping. Moon sees James' black leather warrior jacket on the bed and grabs the red potion. She took at the red position and look at it… thinking, and then she looks at James. She knows that James is right.

Moon opens the bottle and said, "So be it." She drinks the red potion and put the bottle down.

A dark cloud comes and the storm lighting hits.

Moon passed out. James woke up. He noticed that she took the red potion. James feels her pulse and waiting for her to wake up.

Moon passed out. In deep sleep, it felt everything was real. She wakes up in her dream and her father calls her out, "Follow me." She says "dad!"

She follows her dad and finally caught up. Dad and Moon hugged.

Dad told moon, "Not much longer but soon you'll wake up and battle is coming." Moon told dad, "I need you, I can't do this by myself." Dad told moon, "You are special and you have powers now. You'll be able to learn how to control it. You're a strong warrior and this is your destiny to protect people and fight evil." Moon hugs Dad and asked "Will I see you again?"

Dad answered "Yes, but when the time is right. I will always be right beside you in spirit." Moons says, "Goodbye daddy." Dad answered "Goodbye my daughter."

Then Moon woke up and looks at James.

Moon kissed James and hugs him. James tells moon, "I love you." Moon smiled and replied "I love you too, James."

Moon told James, "We have to go now. There's a battle coming. We must warm all Yetis.

James and Moon went back to the village and warned the leader Yeti."

"We must leave now. Rocco and his army knows where we are. I feel him, he's close."

All 12 Yetis and the leader, James and Moon prepared to head out. Just when they started walking, Moon hears a bird making noise, she looks up and sees a black crow, but it was big, a giant crow. It was coming towards her.

Two birds coming at Moon, James steps in front of her and one of the Yeti went in front to protect both of them.

Moon and James took out their swords. All Yeti's roaring and preparing to fight. Towards the hill comes Rocco and his army.

The large three crow birds are going straight to attach Moon but Yeti will not allow that.

Yeti jumps so high, grabs one crow and bites it hard and throw it on the ground.

Moon and James ran away from Rocco and the crows.

Rocco was close enough to use his powers.

He points at Moon, squeeze his hand and he pulls his hand back dragging Moon towards him.

James tried to reach her but it was too late. She was getting pulled back by Rocco's power.

Rocco grabs Moon, holds her neck and choked her. The leader of the Yeti saw Rocco holding moon by the neck. Yeti throws the sparrow and aimed at Rocco. It hit him in the chest. Rocco drops moon.

Moon ran back to James and other Yetis. Rocco takes out the sparrow and tells his army to attack. He stays behind.

Rocco's army attacks Moon, James and 12 Yetis.

Rocco's watching. He calls out "Bangladesh" who he named his favorite crow bird. He says "Snatch moon, take her to the village and keep her pin."

The Bangladesh flew over the attacking Yeti's.

James looks up and saw the giant bird getting close to Moon.

He shouted, "MOON! Look out!"

It was too late. The Bangladesh crow took Moon and flew away. Moon tried to fight the bird but she can't. She held the bird's leg and waits for it to land.

Rocco saw the crow got Moon and vanished. He tells the right man Mawk to tell the army to retreat now.

Sounding the alarm, heading back to the village, James and Yetis have noticed that Moon is gone. James knew the crow bird took her.

James told leader Yeti, "We will get her back and I think I might know where she is."

Leader Yeti told James, "All of us are coming with you. This mountain is no more home." James turned over and looked at the direction Moon might be. Her village that was taken by Rocco.

Bangladesh crow threw moon on the ground and she landed on her back. Moon struggles. Waiting for Rocco to return.

It's getting cold and dark outside. Bangladesh still holding down Moon.

Moon had no choice and couldn't do anything. She has no idea what kind of power she has. She hasn't learn it or discovered what it is.

Rocco returned and saw Moon on the ground, pinned down.

Rocco walked up to his pet bird and gave him a treat.

Two soldiers took Moon up and hold her. Rocco looks at Moon and tells the solder, "Bring her and follow me."

Moon looking around. Rocco taking her to the chamber and sees animals.

Rocco told the solder to tie her up and make sure it's tight.

Rocco tells the soldier "Leave us."

Rocco – "We meet again"

Moon- "The bird is impressive"

Rocco- "I could kill you right now"

Moon- "Then do it already, you have powers"

Rocco- "Why use power on you. I'll kill you adventurously"

Moon- "Seems to me that you want me to be alive longer, why?"

Rocco- "You're right. I do need you alive"

Rocco- "You see, I created something big and there are two more like me as well. You didn't know that. You see I was trained by my father, he never died when your father tried to kill him and stopped him from red diamond."

Moon- "What, your father, he never said anything about him being alive?"

Rocco- "Of course not that he wouldn't have. He thought he killed him. And so he took the red diamond and thinking that, hiding it, would be his best option and not destroying it. My father knew where it was, when I came long, he taught me to be evil and be like him."

Moon- "I came into the picture to destroy you and your father and whoever else is with you, I'll destroy them too."

Rocco laughs and looks at her and says, "Do you think you can defeat me and my father and more of us out there?"

What Rocco doesn't know is that Moon took the red potion that James stole from Rocco.

Moon just needs to know what her powers are and how to use it wisely and control it.

Rocco tells the two soldiers to take Moon and follow him.

Moon wanted to know where Rocco is taking her.

Rocco told moon, "You'll see".

Rocco tells some of his new animals and soldiers, including big foots to follow him.

Moon looking around and tied up, she had no choice but to follow.

Rocco takes moon into the woods along with his armies. His hiding spot for the creature to be released.

Now Rocco wants Moon to see and battle against the creature.

Rocco telling moon, "Are you ready for this. And I want you to fight."

Moon tells Rocco, "If I refuse".

Rocco warns moon, "If you don't fight this creature, I will kill your mom."

Moon looks at Rocco like he knows a lot more about her. She tells him, "Ok I'll do it."

James and 12 Yetis along with 10 Sabertooth hiding in the bushes.

James sees moon standing next to Rocco tied up.

Yeti growling, James tells Yetis and Sabertooth to wait.

Rocco introduce the creature to Moon, "I would like you to meet my very own creation of giant animal you'll see."

Rocco shouts "COME ON OUT, IT IS TIME TO SHOW YOURSELF."

Dark woods in beneath the woods.

Rocco tells Mawk, "Light the fire!"

Moon looks back from her dream and realized this is the dream she was having this moment.

Fire rises, the creature growling making noise trees breaking.

As it was coming, Moon tried to free her hand, Rocco holding her.

Rocco's animals and big foot and his soldiers were backing up slowly. But Moon and Rocco staying still.

All of suddenly trees stop breaking and noise stopped for a few minutes.

A creature jumped out of the bushes, the size of giant elephant, sabertooth. Had red eyes.

Moon looked at the sabertooth and said, "Great."

Sabertooth looks at Rocco and waits for his command.

Rocco tells the sabertooth to fight moon.

Moon looked at Rocco and the sabertooth. Rocco turns over to moon and takes the robe off her wrist. And told her, "Fight or die!"

Rocco gave moon a sword. And prepares to fight the giant sabertooth.

James sees a giant sabertooth. He tells Yeti's and sabertooth to get ready to attack.

Moon and sabertooth head to head.

Sabertooth smacks Moon flying to the ground. Moon falls to the ground, breathing heavily, bleeding through her nose.

James tells "Attack." Moon looks over and sees James. As Yeti's and sabertooth runs to giant sabertooth. Attacking.

Moon tells James, "I need to figure out what my powers are. I need to learn, and be powerful. So I can defeat giant sabertooth and Rocco."

All of the sudden, there was silence. Moon and James looks over and sees the giant sabertooth communicating with small sabertooth.

Moon says, "This is not good." Moon's Sabertooth is now with giant sabertooth command. There are alike and turning against moon.

Moon yells "Run"

James and all yetis are running.

Rocco stood there, Rocco's Bangladesh bird came to him and bowed.

Rocco tells the bird follow Moon, "Return to me and report to me."

The Bangladesh bird took off.

As Moon, James and Yeti were running. They see a waterfall. A cliff. Everyone had no choice but to jump.

The giant sabertooth and small sabertooth returned to their master, Rocco.

Moon, James and all yetis have survived the fall.

Moon told James, "I have to go to the mountain."

James asks "Why?"

Moon – "I left 5 eggs"

James – "Ok but I'm coming with you"

Moon agrees. Moon told the yetis, "Go find a home we will follow your tracks."

Moon and James went back to the mountains. When they returned, they saw Rocco's two soldiers left behind guarding the mountain cave.

James and Moon plan to take them out without being seen.

James had a plan. He told Moon to climb up the tree. "Wait for my call", James told Moon.

Moon waited up on the tree. James went straight to the soldier and said, "Look at me. Come and get me." Two soldiers looked at James and looked at each other. The soldiers ran after James into the woods and saw him standing in the middle of opening. The soldier to take out their sword and walks towards James.

Moon waited for the right moment to jump out of the tree and attack the soldier.

James tells moon, "Now"

Moon jumps out of the tree and kicks the soldier down and helps James fight the other soldier.

After the fight, Moon and James headed to the mountain cave.

She grabs the 5 eggs and puts it in the bag for sage.

James and Moon heads out and follow the trail from Yeti's mark.

As they were walking, they heard a scream of a woman.

Moon and James looked at each other and ran towards the scream.

They hide in the bushes to see what was going on. And sees a beautiful young woman, with brown eyes, brunette hair and average height. She was chained up by different armies. There were 10 soldiers. James and Moon had a good plan.

Moon walked out, walking toward the soldiers in sexy look and said to the leader, "How about you and I head to head for the woman? If I win, I keep the girl. The leader replied "If I win, I keep her and you."

Moon says, "Very well."

Moon looks at the girl and says "She's good and special."

Leader of army name Dwayne

Moon asked questions to the leader of the army named Dwayne "Who are you and where are you from?" Dwayne doesn't answer questions. He does his job what he's told to do.

Moon knew she wasn't going to get any answers.

She takes out her sword and start fighting. James stays put.

Moon stabs in the heart of the leader Dwayne. He fell to the ground. She wins.

She turns around sees 9 soldiers approaching her.

James comes out and stand by moon to fight. The three yeti including leader yeti came back for moon. Sees 9 soldiers getting ready to attack. The yetis jumps out behind moon. And roars. The 9 soldiers looked frightened when they saw the yetis. The soldiers dropped their weapons and ran.

Moon walks towards the girl and asked her name.

The girl says, "My name is Emmie"

Moon says, "My name is Moon and this is James."

"Don't be afraid this is the leader Yeti. The yetis are with me… Good ones. They won't hurt you", Moon said.

Moon told James to give her water.

Moon asked her, "What happened to you?"

Molly- "I was captured by scary man. He had black long coat and he had red eyes and powers. He destroyed my home, killed my family, I have nowhere else to go."

Moon told her, "You can come with us. When we see a next village. We will drop you off there."

James takes Moon way from her to talk to her.

James – "We can't take her, we don't have time."

Moon - "Look at her, she needs us. Don't make me leave her behind.

You heard her she has no one."

James said "Ok"

Moon told James, "I'll keep an eye on her."

Moon walked up to Emmie and said, "You're coming with us. Emmie was excited and she told Moon, "You won't regret it."

James, Moon and Molly follows Yeti.

It was a long way walk. They all finally made it. Leader Yeti said, "This can be our new home, not much but at least for now."

Moon told yeti, "It will do".

Moon ask leader yeti to train her to get ready for Rocco.

Yeti agrees and said, "At dawn, we will start training."

Moon walks away and heads to the woods. She needed her own time and figured out her powers that has been bothering her.

Moon sits down, cross her legs, hands on her knee and closes her eyes. Asking for her father to help her what her powers are and how to use it. "Show me what my powers are father. I can't do this, I need you father."

Moon heard a whisper. She opens her eyes and didn't see anything but hear voice.

The voice told her to follow the path and go straight. She followed the path and goes straight.

As she walked 5 miles. She sees a land and a small house with trees around it.

She goes up to the door, knocks but no answer. She knocks again and the door crack open.

Entering slowly into the house, dark, dusty and candles burning.

She stands in the middle of the circle and sees a shadow walking toward.

She yells, "Who's there?"

A woman she's dressed in a warrior comes out of the shadow.

Moon questions her, "Who are you? And what do you want from me?"

A woman in white long coat with a hood in the shadow faces Moon.

She pulls out her hood and says, "My name is Molly, the queen she's my mother."

Moon looked at and said, the queen never told me she had a daughter.

Molly – "Yes I know. My mother made it a secret that she has a daughter. She didn't want anyone to find out. But when I found out my mother died. And there's a new queen to take her place. I had to know who is queen."

Moon – "I am the queen, the keeper, the warrior. I was with your mom when she died. She was brave and wanted me to take over. To destroy the red diamond."

Molly continued "The red diamond has been destroyed but not the evil. He's still alive and has powers. Long story but short. I have powers but I don't know what is it yet or how to use it.

Molly says, "My queen, it would be owner to fight beside you all the way"

Moon bowed her head and took her as a second partner.

Molly can sense Moon has power.

Molly asked moon, "Do you know powers?"

Moon – "No but how do you know I have powers?"

Molly – "I can sense and I can see right through you."

Moon – "I need your help I don't know what my powers are."

Molly – "Moon come sit down the floor."

Molly and Moon sits down cross each other.

Molly puts a cup with water in the middle.

She tells moon to close her eyes.

Molly says "Go deep into the mind… What do you see?"

Moon answered "I see me standing, in the woods."

Molly asked, "What do you see in front of you?"

Moon answered "I'm moving things with my mind and lifting rocks and keeping it steady."

Molly – "That's it keep going."

Moon looking into her mind and sees what her powers are.

She opened her eyes and looked down at the glass. With her mind she can do anything lift, throw. And with her hand she can do the same thing. As she uses her powers she gets stronger.

She looks at Molly and says "Thank you." Molly and Moon went outside to go to the rest of the group.

When they returned. Leader yeti and James looked at this new person who is with moon.

James – "Who is this?"

Moon – "This is Molly. The queen's daughter."

James get fire started and cooks food. Moon talks to yeti about tomorrow, "I want you to train tomorrow."

Yeti will train moon at dawn.

They all gather around the fire. Moon speaks to all of them.

"We need to keep moving. Rocco is one step ahead. Only I will fight him, no one else. Tomorrow yeti will train all of you. We all have to be prepared. James you must go ahead of us, find many armies. We will need them. I will gather the animals. Molly we are in the middle of a war. We could use this extra person."

Molly says to moon, "It would be my honor to serve you."

Moon told everyone, "We must all rest up, tomorrow is a big day."

Leader of yeti wakes up and wakes moon up.

Moon and yeti goes into the open grass field.

Yeti trained Moon and Moon learned everything.

Moon also showed yeti her powers.

Yeti saw and was proud of Moon.

Yeti said – "You're ready. I taught you everything you need to learn."

Moon bowed down for the leader of yeti. Yeti told her, "Get up. You don't need to bow to me. I bow to you."

Yeti bowed down and told her, "I will always protect you until death."

They both headed back to the rest of the group.

Moon noticed that James wasn't there but left her a note. It says, "My dear queen, I left at midnight. I'm going to get more armies and more creatures. We will see each other again."

As they head out looking for Rocco and to fight.

Rocco and all his armies have gotten stronger.

Rocco told Mawk to tell the armies and the animals to get ready to leave as they are going to attack Moon.

Rocco went into the woods to get the creature named Sabertooth, size of elephant and rest of small sabertooth. He unleashed the anaconda and big foots, tigers and bears.

Rocco came back with lots of animals and shouted, "We aregoing to war. This is it!"

Rocco moves out with his armies.

Moon and theothers have already headed out.

Moon starts to feel the bag shaking. There were eggs 2 headed snakes.

She told the others to hold up. Molly told her, "What's up?"

Moon – "It's my bag, I think the eggs are cracking."

Moon told Molly, "Your mother, the queen saved these eggs and protected it. I took it and kept it safe. Rocco who is evil took our village."

Moon took out 5 eggs and lay them down into the ground.

The eggs starts to crack open.

Moon tells everyone to back up, "I don't think this is going to be good."

They all backed up and waited for the 2 headed snakes to come out.

It was tiny snakes but then it started to grow big.

Moon told everyone not to move.

All 5, 2 headed snakes grew of the size like a giraffe. The snakes were aggressive and testing them.

Moon told Emmy not to move but she was so scared. She starts to run.

The 2 headed snakes attack her and swallowed her.

Moon used her power to get the snake to listen to her and that she is the boss control of the snake.

Moon told Molly and all yeti, "Stay still. Do not move a muscle."

Moon walks up to the snake and says, "You are my creature. You listen to me." The snake circled around moon and she is in the middle.

The snake spoke, only moon can understand and talk to animals.

The moon tells the snake, "The first queen died and she pass it on to me to be the queen, warrior. We are going to war."

The snake didn't listen to her. The snake opened its mouth starts to get close to moon's head. Moon starts to use her powers.

Moon closed her eyes and using her mind to make the snake in the air.

She opens her eyes. Eye to eye.

One snake floating up in the air. The 7other 4 snakes looked and backed off.

Moon drops the snake to the ground hard.

She walks toward the snake and says, "You will follow me, you are under my command."

5 snakes, starts to follow the queen. Knowing that she has powers made them realized.

Preparing for war. Both sides have left their home and laned. Moon and Rocco both have powers.

It was getting dark, Moon told Molly, "We will camp here for the night. Yetis went to look for sticks."

Molly and Moon went to check out further to the woods and made sure no one followed and it's safe.

As they camp for the night, Moon and Molly talk for a while. Figuring out a plan.

Moon walked toward the fire and lied down and went to sleep.

While everyone is sleeping, Rocco sees smoke up ahead, he told Mauk to take some soldiers and check it out.

Moon woke up and sense a danger coming.

She woke others up and left the fire burning.

They hide in the woods for cover.

Surely it's Roccos armies.

Moon had a plan, she told molly, "We're going to follow them. Bring us to Rocco."

She signs yetis and Molly. They have plan.

Rocco's armies sees camp site and looked around nothing but they knew someone has been here.

They all turn around and head back.

Moon's group followed them but far a distance.

The sun was rising, day light.

They saw an open land up ahead and lots of armies.

Moon and Molly and her yetis and the snakes. Moon hearing Rocco's voice. Rocco's telling to move out.

Moon didn't want lose him.

This was an opportunity to fight him.

Molly says to moon, "I'll stay right beside you." Moon looks at yetis and the snakes.

The leader yeti told moon, "I'm with you all the way."

Moon – "Together we fight!"

Moon turned around and saw Rocco and his armies moving out of the land heading up the hill.

Moon jumps out of the bushes and yells "ROCCO!"

Rocco stops and all his armies and animals have stopped. Turns around and sees moon

Rocco – "Well well well Moon. What a surprise."

Rocco's armies were getting ready to attack her until Moon's armies came out of the bushes.

Rocco saw more of her armies. Rocco knows he has more.

But he notice she has 7 headed snakes and 5 of them the size of giraffe.

Rocco put his hands up and told his armies not to attack yet.

Rocco told Mauk, Whatever happens to me. You take over and keep attacking. I told you everything about my father and where to go if you're unable to win. My father will help you. You still have more to learn."

Rocco walks front of the middle of the circle of the land.

Moon also walks front the middle of the circle of the land.

Eye to eye. Rocco and Moon takes out the sword.

Rocco – "Two-headed snake, impressive

Moon – "Thank you!"

Rocco – Rocco calls out release his cobra snake.

Moon – sees the cobra snake. Bigger than 2 headed snake.

Rocco – "Let's see what my snake can do with your snake."

Moon's 2 headed snakes are going crazy and aggressive towards Rocco's cobra.

One of hers starts to swirl on to the land and heading straight to the cobra. Cobra charges the 2 headed snake.

Biting, attacking, bloody.

Moon seeing her 2 head snake losing. Both side watching. Seeing black cobra pinning down her snake

She used her hand to lift cobra in the air and throw it at Rocco's armies.

Rocco was shock, saw moon has powers and got angry and starts to swing his sword. Moon ducked and swing her sword, both sword touching together like an x, face to face. Dark grey clouds comes both side. Thunder, lighting hits on Moon and Rocco's sword attach together. Like giving them more powers.

Moon kicks Rocco back. And yells attack!!

Both sides starts to attack.

Moon and Rocco fighting. Moon grabs her knife in her boot pulls it out and stab him on his shoulder. He swings his wrist and hits her face.

Moon falls down to the ground, nose bleeding. She stands back up and Rocco use his power on her. Blew her further out. Rocco calls his bird.

Moon gets back up and runs toward Rocco. Didn't realized he called his bird for help. She runs, behind her, Rocco's bird picks up moon and flying with the bird. Moon grabs the knife same time trying to find landing.

Leader yeti and Molly saw moon getting captured by big crow bird.

They fall her heading straight into the woods tree.

Moon stabbing the bird to release her and being low enough to land on the ground. The bird was injured.

Released moon and landed on her two feet. Sees the bird dropped to the ground. She walks up to the bird and stabs the bird on the head.

Molly and leader yeti they were happy she didn't go far or got hurt.

Moon looked at Molly and yeti let's go back. We can't let Rocco disappear.

As they were heading back, James saw moon and called out her name.

Moon turns around and saw James with a lot of armies and animals.

She ran and hugged James and said, "It's good to see you."

Moon was please and said, "Follow me."

Running back to the field and sees armies both sides and animals fighting each other.

Moon sees Rocco trying to leave and leaving his armies behind. Moon would not allow him to leave.

Everyone looked at the direction of Moon and James coming with bunch of armies and animals coming at them.

Moon running after Rocco. As she got closer she threw a knife at his leg to slow him down. Rocco dropped to the ground with Moon's knife on his leg. Pulls it out and gets back up and prepare using power.

Moon using her powers. Both had no idea they had a weapon call lighting strike for their hands.

Both takes their hand out aiming at each other out came lighting together tight trying to strike.

Moon and Rocco head to head strike lighting. Moon didn't know she had this power. Holding it together.

Moon starting to feel weak because she hasn't used her powers a lot.

With her left hand controlling strike lighting at Rocco's lighting. She use her right hand sword and throw it at his heart fast.

The sword went into his heart. Rocco falls on his knee and take the sword out. Moon going up to him and thinking he's dead.

She picks up the sword. And turns around Rocco faking gets up and gets ready to stab her.

James seeing Rocco getting ready to stab her. James yelled so loud to Moon and Moon turned around and saw Rocco standing with the sword.

Rocco stabbed Moon in the stomach.

Moon taking her breath and looking at him. Rocco telling Moon before her last breath. "You should have cut my head off. I can't die." Rocco takes the sword out of her stomach and falls to the ground. Lying there bleeding still alive.

James ran into Rocco fighting him for revenge.

Yeti saw Moon to the ground not moving. Battle still going on.

One of Rocco's anaconda coming straight for Moon.

Yeti saw the anaconda heading straight at moon and tells 2 headed snake roaring for Moon in danger.

Yeti and 2 headed snake running towards Moon.

Anaconda starts to stand tall and getting ready to swallow moon.

2 headed snake swirled fast at anaconda and attacking each other.

Yeti cared Moon and bring her to a safe spot. Yeti tearing roaring.

Yeti looking at the armies and roaring anger. Molly sees Moon lying there not moving.

Molly told yeti, "Don't worry." Molly takes out a potion and opens her mouth and gave her a potion."

Yeti and Molly looking at wound and healing. Moon's eyes open and breaths. She looks at Molly and says, "Thank you for saving my life." Molly smiled and yeti excited. Moon gets up sees Rocco still alive and sees him and James fighting. Rocco takes James to the ground and pin him down. Has his sword by James neck.

Moon taking her sword and walks behind him. As Rocco prepares to stab James, Moon swings her sword at Rocco's neck and chops his head off.

Rocco's head came off his body fell to the ground. James seeing moon alive. Gets up and kiss her.

Rocco's armies stopped fighting and looked at Rocco's body. Moon says "It's over. Go back where you came from or war will still continue. I'm giving you a chance to walk away and live."

Molly, James, and yeti standing next to moon. James says. "It's over we did it."

Moon says, "No it's not over yet. I have to do one more thing."

Moon told them, "I have to do this alone."

James wouldn't allow that. He says to moon, "Wherever you go, we go."

Moon shared one more thing. She told James and Molly, yeti too.

When she was captured from Rocco, Rocco has father and he's behind all this.

James told moon, "I'm coming with you. And that's final." Yeti and Molly would not stay behind."

All 4 starts to head out.

James asked Moon, "Do you know where you're going?"

Moon – "Yes I do. And I know where the castle IS. When Rocco kept me in the chamber. He told me everything."

I saw a map and it had castle on the map. I took the map.

After walking few hours, they came across a bridge, a long bridge.

James went first to test it, check it out.

He returns and looked safe. He told everyone to go one by one.

Moon went first and crossed the bridge. Moon heard noise in the woods. She heads straight into the woods. She saw Rocco's large sabertooth.

Moon's friends crossed the bridge and finds her into the bushes.

James gets closer to Moon and ducks like her. He saw Rocco's sabertooth.

James tells moon, "You can't defeat large sabertooth."

Moon – "I have powers."

James – "Your powers didn't work before."

Moon – "That's because I didn't know how to use it."

James – "What if it doesn't work on sabertooth?"

Moon – "There's only one way to find out."

Moon gets out of the bushes and yells "HEY!"

Sabertooth turned around and roars.

Moon stead still, James and Molly, yeti runs to Moon and stands with her.

James tells Moon to use her powers now.

Moon uses her powers from her hand. She tried to put sabertooth in the air. Didn't work.

Moon looks at James and told Him, "My power doesn't work on sabertooth.

James – "I told you."

Moon – "Well it was worth a try."

James – "We need to figure out how to destroy giant sabertooth . It's powerful"

Moon had an idea. She told Molly James and yeti. To back up and make room and stay still.

Moon yells at sabertooth and waved and took out her small knife and threw it at sabertooth face.

Moon – "Everybody stay still, I got a plan."

Moon runs back toward the bridge and cliffs.

She stops turns and waits for sabertooth.

Sabertooth roaring charges at her. Moon runs follows the cliff. Going straight out an opening field surrounded by cliffs.

She takes out her sword. Eye to eye.

Moon tried to fight Sabertooth.

Sabertooth using his paw pushes her down. Pins her down. She drops her sword. Pin down. Sabertooth opening his mouth with giant tooth.

Moon looks over at her sword reaching for it. She sees her 2 headed snakes 2 of them swirling and bites sabertooth on the back wrap around to pin sabertooth down.

Moon gets up and backs up. Watching 2 headed snake kill sabertooth.

Sabertooth bites one and throws it. The other wraps around the neck and bites his head. Down came Sabertooth bleeding out.

The snakes went up to moon to protect her.

James and Molly, yeti running to moon.

Molly – "Are you ok?"

Moon – "I am now"

Moon – "My plan was to throw sabertooth off the cliff."

Molly – "I thought that was your plan."

Moon smiled at Molly.

Moon – now that sabertooth is dead. We have to get to the castle.

James asked Moon, what about 2 headed snakes.

Moon – "They're coming with us. They can be useful."

Moon told others, she's only there to kill Rocco's father. It's for my father.

My father never killed him. He thought winning by getting Red diamond and hiding it would do the trick and having peace would do it.

Moon looks to the right and saw up head castle, Dark cloud over the castle.

Moon and the others head out, going straight to the castle.

She gets closer to the castle and hide.

She needed a plan. She told James, Molly to split up.

Moon and yeti climbed up. Saw an open window.

Moon and yeti looking for Rocco's father.

Moon hears animals roaring in the chamber. She walks down into the chamber. Dark, cold. Sense of evil.

She lit the fire and went further in. Yeti right beside her. Yeti sniffing and breathing heavenly.

Moon looked at yeti told him "it's ok."

Moon sees bars and each bars has animals in them.

Tigers, Lions, black bears and many more. Up a head one special hidden door. She goes toward the door. Trying to see what's inside. To dark and quite.

Animals making noise. She turns animals going crazy.

All of sudden, it got quite. Moon and yeti leaves and continue.

Molly and James found Moon.

One soldier spotted Moon and sounded alarm. Moon recognized this soldier before. She let him go and ran off. Didn't know he was working for Rocco's father.

Moon takes out her sword and throws it at the soldier while he was sounding the alarm.

More soldiers coming. James told Moon to run.

Moon didn't want to leave them behind.

The soldiers captured James, yeti and Molly. Moon ran to hide.

Moon followed them, hoping to bring her to Rocc'os father.

One of the soldier speaks to Rocc'os father, name is thrown. Soldiers speaks to thrown and brings Molly, James and yeti in. Moon finally saw who Rocco's father and his name.

Thrown question the girl Molly.

Where is moon?

Molly – "S you know who she is."

Thrown – "I know everything, my son I taught him very well to be like me."

Molly – "About your son. I hate to say but he's dead."

Thrown – "No he's not dead he will return, he always does."

Moon had an idea. She had go back where Rocco died and hopefully his body is there still.

Thrown says to his body guard to take James and Molly into dungeon

One of the soldier asked Thrown, "What about this one?"

Thrown – "Yes this one, you must be yeti the leader." Yeti roaring, Thrown tells soldier, "Take him to the chamber along with the animals."

Thrown – "The rest of you, find Moon, she's around. And bring her to me unharmed."

Moon headed back to Rocco. She saw the body still there. Grabs the head and puts it in the bag. She uses her powers on 3 soldiers standing guarding outside the door.

Moon walks into the castle and takes out her sword, fighting.

She calls out her 2 headed snake.

The snake comes in, Moon tells the snake, "Run the solders over. Kill what ever is in the way." The snake does what moon wants her to do.

Moon walks behind the snake, staying behind the snake.

She enters, and saw Thrown sitting in his chair.

Thrown – "Very clever".

The snake hiss at thrown.

Surrounded by many soldiers and trapped. She didn't care, because she knew she has powers and could use it anytime.

Moon tells to Thrown asked where the three of her own people are.

Thrown tells his solders to go and get the three prisoners. And bring them here. And then whispers in his ear to release the animals including human creature red door.

Thrown question Moon asked her what's in the bag.

Moon – "You'll see."

Moon looks over to the right and saw the soldiers bringing Molly, James and yeti.

She looks back at thrown tells him, "Your son, his name is Rocco. I'm sure you heard a lot about me."

Thrown tells moon, "Rocco my son will return, he can't die."

Moon – "I wish that was true. But unfortunately your son is dead."

Thrown – Stood up with angry tone SILENTS!

Moon takes out the head and throws it at Thrown.

Thrown looks down and saw the head of his son.

Moon drops the bag and takes out the sword and says. I have killed your son and now I'm going to kill you.

Soldiers getting ready to attack her but Thrown said, "No she's mine."

Thrown can think what moon is thinking. Moon using her powers on thrown. Thrown uses his powers.

Moon was shock. Thrown tells moon, "You're not the only one with powers."

Here comes animals and a giant human with 4 hands and with half face that was behind red door.

Moon looks up and tried to use her powers but it was too big.

Thrown comes at Moon and swings his sword at her hard and fast.

The giant half face human with 4 hands coming at Moon. James and yeti has they partner up throws at giant half face. And finally got the creatures attention.

Moon and thrown fighting using powers.

Blood everywhere and creatures everywhere.

Moon slice Thrown's arm. Thrown backs up and looks at her. He starts to run away from her.

Moon heard James yelling. She went over to help yeti and James. She grabs the robe. And throws it at giant half face. Legs and junk it to ground. Falls down and yeti jumps on pin it down. James with his sword.

Pushes the sword into the heart.

Molly runs to moon. Molly said, "Did you kill Thrown?"

Moon – "No he ran away. I'm going to hunt him down."

Molly – "Coming with you. Ok"

James – me too.

Moon told yeti to go back with his people. And said. We will see each other again.

Moon, James and Molly took off to go find thrown.

Thrown running into the forest.

Moon and two more running, catching up on him.

Moon dives and lands on Thrown, falls to the grown. Thrown using his powers on Moon's friends.

Moon using her sword to fight. Thrown grabs her neck and lifts her up. James sneaks behind thrown back and stabs him and drops moon.

Thrown turns around grabs James.

Moon grabs her sword and swings cuts his head off.

Molly and Moon looked at each other and was happy it's over.

Molly – "Should we head back to the castle?"

Moon – "No how about you and James and I start a new adventure and move on? Three of us."

Moon – "I have to stop one place."

James and Molly follows Moon.

Moon went back home to go see her mother.

She made it home and saw the door has been broken and inside been destroyed. She looks around to see any evidence or marks.

James and Molly told her we will find your mom.

All of sudden. A man calls out

Moon! Moon I know you're in there. Come on out.

Moon looking threw the window, saw her mom tide up and taped on her mouth.

Seeing three strange men. Moon doesn't know them.

She comes out with James and Molly

Moon says to the man, what's your name. My name is Roll. And I'm going to be taking this home and your village.

Moon tells Roll. Never going to happen. Release my mother.

Roll wasn't going to do that. Molly and James and Moon takes out the sword preparing to fight.

Roll pushing moons mom to ground.

Moon sees her 2 headed snake coming behind Roll.

Moon puts her sword away, Molly told her, what you are doing. It's ok Molly. You will not need to fight.

Roll sees that moon put her sword away and said to Roll.

I don't need to fight you or your two men.

Roll – you're making this way to easy.

James and Molly was looking at moon like she's not herself. But then they hear hisses sound. And realized. Moon was going to have the snake get them.

Roll – takes out his sword and prepared to fight moon while she down guard.

2 headed snake 2 of them standing tall behind three men

Roll hears hissing behind him and turns around. 2 headed snake swallows three men.

Moon told the snakes. Well done

Moon runs over to her mom and unties her and takes the tape off her mouth.

Mom was happy to see her daughter Moon. All grown up and dress in black warrior, Strong women.

Moon's mom got scared of 2 headed snake.

Moon told her mom it's ok. There not going to hurt you.

Mom showed Moon where her father's is buried. She went over for he stone of her father and put a flower next to the stone. And says, father it is done. The red diamond as destroyed along with Rocco and thrown, Rocco father. May you be in piece? I miss so much father.

Moon walks back to her mom and sees Molly and James standing over by 2 headed snakes.

Moon tells her mom. I have to go now. And do what I do save more people. Are you going to be ok? Her mom told her daughter. Of course my daughter and I'm so proud of you. Your father would be very happy.

Moon smiles and Hughes her mom. We will see each other again.

Take care yourself my daughter. You too mom.

Moon goes to James and molly.

Moon – I don't know where we go from you. But we are a team. Stick together and a new adventure begins.

Moon goes up to 2 headed snakes and told the snakes. You are free. Go, go now.

The snakes took off.

Moon, James, and Molly took off and sees a village up a head. It was getting dark.

They enter the villages and walks in.

They sees people drinking and dancing, parting.

They got a table, sat down ordered drinks

Moon made a toast. Molly and James thank you for staying by me and fighting. And glad we met. James and Molly drink to that.

James asked Moon, what's next, where we go from here.

Moon told James and Molly. We are going to stick together. And continue a journey. A new journey.

James picks up his drink and looks at Moon says. A new journey together

Molly picks up her drink and looks at Moon says, a new journey together

Moon picks up her drink and together. All three drinks and decide to stay for the night.

Moon gets up along with her two others. They grab what they need and sees a path.

Moon looks over at Molly and James, Moon tells them. Are you ready? Both said. We are ready as will ever be.

Moon, James and Molly as they head off and continue their new adventure Moon also spotted a beautiful white horse. The horse was stuck in the mud. Moon grabs her robe and threw it around horse neck. Got the horse out of the mud and said. You'll be my horse and call you spirit.

The creatures of moons have gone to their own world and yeti has gone back to his home mountain. Two headed snakes found a home.

The rest we will never find out.

The End

CPSIA information can be obtained
at www.ICGtesting.com
Printed in the USA
LVHW040134270320
651353LV00002BA/493